Adventure in the Lost World

BY R.W. STROH

Illustrated by Kim Mulkey

TROLL ASSOCIATES

Library of Congress Cataloging in Publication Data

Stroh, R.W.
 Adventure in the lost world.

 Summary: In the role of a sailor gone three years
from home, the reader is asked by a mysterious stranger
to return to help his/her parents, then chooses the turns
of a plot full of monstrous adventures.
 1. Plot-your-own stories.   2. Children's stories.
[1. Fantasy.   2. Plot-your-own stories]   I. Mulkey,
Kim, ill.   II. Title.
PZ7.S9215Ad   1985   [Fic]   85-2530
ISBN 0-8167-0535-6 (lib. bdg.)
ISBN 0-8167-0536-4 (pbk.)

10   9   8   7   6   5   4   3   2   1

We Hope You Enjoy
This Adventure Story

Just remember to read it differently than you would most other books. Start on page 1 and keep reading till you come to a choice. After that the story is up to you. Your decisions will take you from page to page.

Think carefully before you decide. Some choices will lead you to exciting, heroic, and happy endings. But watch out! Other choices can quickly lead to disaster.

Now you are ready to begin. The best of luck in your adventure!

It has been three years since you left home to become a sailor. No one from your faraway village thought you would succeed. But you quickly learned the ropes, and now you can climb the rigging as fast as any old salt.

Tonight you are having dinner with your friends at the Red Ox Inn. After dinner, an old man in a gray cloak draws you aside and tells you some unexpected news.

There has been trouble at home, and your parents badly need your help. He won't say more than that, but he does tell you to be careful. Strange men have been asking questions about you at the town gate.

You know of a ship leaving for your home port in one hour. But the old man tells you not to take this ship—you may never reach home. He advises you to take the old forest road, and to leave town as soon as possible.

If you want to take the ship home, turn to page 2.

If you want to take the old forest road home, turn to page 4.

If you want to spend the night at the inn and wait till morning, turn to page 6.

You decide to take the ship, and hurry down to the dock. Luckily Captain Butler needs one more deckhand. He hires you on the spot. You sleep on the ship tonight in your own cozy hammock.

You are only out at sea a few days when the wind dies. One day goes by without a breeze, then another. The crew begins to grumble, then argue. After two more days of calm pass, a mutiny breaks out. Captain Butler, his three mates, and several sailors are put on a small lifeboat. There may be an island nearby.

Now mutiny leader James Coffin asks you to decide for yourself. Whom do you want to join? The mutineers? Or the men in the boat? Everyone is waiting for your decision.

If you want to join the mutineers, turn to page 16.

If you want to join the men in the lifeboat, turn to page 20.

You give Leda your ring. She leads you to a small cove. There is a sailboat, supplied with food and fresh water. She even gives you a map.

You thank her and begin your journey again.

You have not sailed far before the same unidentified ship spots your small boat and sails over to you.

Turn to page 53.

4

from page 1 / from page 45

You leave through a little-used gate at the edge of town. A dirt road takes you toward your home.

It is very late and you are getting tired. You don't want to meet any strangers all by yourself on this lonely road. It would be much safer to travel by day.

You find a well-hidden spot off the road, and sleep under the stars.

As soon as dawn breaks, you follow the road again. Soon the road comes to a fork. The right fork leads to the mountains, the left to a forest.

If you want to take the mountain path, turn to page 30.

If you want to take the forest path, turn to page 28.

The frost giants plan to cook you for their supper. They take you back to their camp. Suddenly you hear a small voice. "I know where you can find tastier dishes."

"What?" says one of the giants. "Where?"

"Down by the lake."

Frost giants are not very clever. These three look at each other, and you can almost hear them thinking: "One person is not enough for three of us to eat."

They leave you in the sack and rumble down to the lake. As soon as they are gone, you feel the sack being loosened. It is the fox.

"I suggest you get away quickly," says the fox. "And thank you again."

With that the fox bounds away into the gathering dusk.

You dash into the forest. Night is coming quickly, and you don't want to get lost. Trying to find a path, you climb up a short hill to have a look around. You see nothing.

You are just about to walk back down the hill when you are surrounded by slim people clad in oak leaves.

Turn to page 17.

from page 1

Right now a good night's sleep is what you need most. But you take the old man's warning about strange men seriously. You prop a heavy chair against the door, and sleep fully clothed.

The full moon lights your room. From your second-story window, you see the ship that will leave for your home port in a few minutes. You can always catch another in a few days.

In the northeast, you see forests and mountains rising in the distance.

Just before you go to sleep, you hear your door handle squeak. You don't waste time asking who is there.

Turn to page 45.

You begin to smash the door with axes and swords.

Zap! You are all changed into toads and salamanders. It may not be such a bad life, if you enjoy eating insects.

THE END

You enter the island forest. Birds and insects chatter. But as you walk uphill, the trees thin out and the animals suddenly grow quiet.

Then you hear human voices. Peeking from behind one of the trees, you see pirates! They are standing around a big hole, arguing bitterly.

Turn to page 25.

You don't like the idea of attacking a wizard head-on. So you join the two others to try to find a back entrance. Suddenly you see an amazing sight at the edge of the forest. A unicorn!

The unicorn is so beautiful, you know it can't be a trick. The two soldiers forget all about their mission, and run toward the unicorn. They want to capture it.

If you want to help the soldiers, turn to page 21.

If you want to help the unicorn, turn to page 82.

You give the helmet to Aleric, and he can barely control his excitement. Together you go to the wizard's castle. Aleric commands the wizard to leave the valley forever. The curse is lifted!

But now there is a new curse. Aleric takes over the castle and becomes an even more ruthless ruler in the wizard's place.

THE END

You don't trust the gleam in Aleric's eyes, so you keep the helmet. With the helmet, it is easy to force the wizard to lift the spell and to leave the valley forever.

Now the village is freed, and the castle stands empty. What will you do with the powerful helmet?

If you want to destroy the helmet, so it can never be used again, turn to page 62.

If you want to hide the helmet, turn to page 67.

You don't know whether you can trust Leda, so you keep walking along the beach. You never meet another person on the island, but you do find delicious fruits and small wild animals.

You build yourself a tree house, and live the rest of your life on this island paradise.

THE END

You free the fox. Remarkably, his leg does not appear to be injured. He thanks you and goes on his way. You walk all day and get quite tired. You are not paying attention when three frost giants catch you and put you in their sack.

Turn to page 5.

from page 2

You hate to join the mutineers, but you don't think you would survive long in the lifeboat on the open sea.

You agree to join James Coffin and his crew, hoping they will finish the trip to your home port. Unfortunately, they have no such intention. Coffin and his men decide to become pirates. They are going to raid a small village on the coast.

You want nothing to do with this raid, but you can't jump overboard in the middle of the ocean.

The night of the raid, the mutineers anchor their ship just outside the harbor. They will attack in three hours, in the quietest hour of the night.

Suddenly, a sailor takes you aside.

"I don't care what James Coffin does with this ship," says the sailor, "but he has no right to harm innocent people. I'm going to swim for shore to warn the village. I could use your help. Will you join me?"

You are a good swimmer, and the shore is only about one mile away.

If the mutineers catch you, however, you can expect no mercy from them.

If you want to swim and warn the village, turn to page 50.

If you do not want to risk it, turn to page 46.

from page 21

You have read about leafers in storybooks, but you never thought you would meet any. You wish you knew more about these good creatures. So far, not one of them has said a word. They are staring at you calmly.

You begin to speak to them, and soon tell the whole story about your journey.

After listening to you carefully, one of the leafers finally speaks:

"It is dangerous for you to continue walking in the forest. There is much evil here. The road to the mountain is the way you must go to get home. We can tell you how to get there.

"However, we have a favor to ask of you. We could use your help—to get rid of an ogre. Will you please help us? You are under no obligation. We will direct you to the mountain road in any case."

If you want to help the leafers, turn to page 43.

If you accept their directions and go to the mountain, turn to page 30.

You do not trust the fox, so you keep walking through the woods. The trees grow taller, the leaves thicker. Little light seeps through. By the end of the day you are tired. You are not paying attention when three frost giants nab you and put you in their sack.

There is no one to call for help.

THE END

from page 2

James Coffin and the crew have broken the law. You decide to try your luck with Captain Butler. You begin to row. A day passes, and luck is with you. In the distance, on the right, you spot a tropical island. On the left sails a three-masted ship that is not flying any flag.

A storm is gathering behind you.

If you want to row for the island, turn to page 24.

If you want to row for the ship, turn to page 53.

from page 10

The unicorn runs lightly into the forest. You all chase it. Soon you and the soldiers wander in different directions. You all become quite lost in the woods. It may be a while before you find your way out.

THE END

from page 87

You throw water on their light, and it goes out with a hiss. Now the huffers howl in fright. They can't see anything in the dark. But you and Baldur can see perfectly. You make short work of the foul huffers.

After they all lie dead, you search the room further. You find treasure. One hundred gold pieces for each of you.

"This is a good day's work," says Baldur. Together you find a safe tunnel to the other side of the mountain. You are on your way home.

THE END

from page 20

You do not trust an unmarked ship on the high seas, so you row quickly for the island. But the storm is upon you. Winds blow, and large waves rock your small boat. You are in a tropical storm. Suddenly you are swept overboard.

You wash up on shore, unharmed but alone. There is no sign of your fellow sailors.

You wonder if the island is inhabited.

If you want to walk inland through a forest, turn to page 9.

If you want to walk along the beach, turn to page 33.

from page 9

Suddenly the pirates get into a terrible fight. One of them is killed, and another is bound and left leaning against a tree. The remaining pirates bury a wooden chest in the soft earth. Then they creep away into the forest.

After they are gone, you walk slowly into the clearing. The bound man wears tattered clothes. He is unconscious.

If you want to untie the man and try to revive him, turn to page 31.

If you want to dig up the wooden chest, turn to page 36.

26

You take the left, warmer tunnel. Suddenly four huffers jump into view. Your light must have attracted these vicious creatures of the mountains. Now they are coming for you. Their jagged swords sparkle in the torch light.

You will have to fight for your lives.

Turn to page 63.

from page 4

You have not walked far into the forest when you hear the small cry of an animal. It is a fox, with its leg caught in a trap. "Won't you please free me?" asks the fox.

If you want to free the fox, turn to page 15.

If you want to keep on walking, turn to page 18.

"That is wonderful," you say. "But I don't think you can turn into an ogre."

"Of course I can," he says. He turns into an ugly ogre.

"An ogre! Amazing!" you say. "But I have heard that you can only turn into monsters, not into something ordinary like a mouse."

"Fool." Lokrin easily turns into a common field mouse. You grab the mouse and put it into a small sack. Then you take the helmet for your own.

"Excellent work," says Aleric. "Now give me the helmet. Then I can defeat the wizard and anyone else who dares to get in our way."

If you want to give the helmet to Aleric, turn to page 11.

If you want to keep the helmet yourself, turn to page 12.

30

from page 4 / from page 17 / from page 88

You climb a narrow path up the mountain. At first it is difficult. Vines and thorns slow you down and tear at your clothing. Then the trail becomes easier.

You are halfway up the mountain when you come to an impasse. Some kind of rock slide has completely blocked the way.

Then you see what has caused the slide. Stone giants are hurling rocks from above, and you see some of the rocks tumbling toward you. Your only escape is a small cave in the side of the mountain. You run inside as an avalanche seals up the entrance behind you.

Turn to page 40.

from page 25

You untie the man and revive him. His name is John Starbuck, and he is a brave sailor who was captured by the pirates and left here to die with the treasure. Together you climb to the highest point of the island. You spot a passing Royal Navy ship, and signal it with a smoky fire.

The pirates are captured. You and Starbuck share a generous reward from the buried treasure chest, and the Navy ship gives you a ride home.

THE END

33

from page 24

You walk along the beach, but see no sign of the unmarked ship or your companions. Then you hear a voice.

"Oh, dear, another shipwrecked sailor."

You turn and meet a sea spirit, sitting on a rock. "My name is Leda," she says. "I can help you get home. All I ask in return is a present from you—that beautiful silver ring on your finger."

The ring is your last possession.

If you want to give the ring to Leda, turn to page 3.

If you want to walk inland, turn to page 9.

If you want to continue walking along the beach, turn to page 13.

from page 87

You run for the door, but the huffers can run just as fast as you. They catch you, and bring you and Baldur back to their terrible dungeon.

THE END

You go along with Captain Smith for now, and hope you get a chance to escape later. Anything is better than walking the plank.

"Excellent choice," says Captain Smith. "I knew you would see reason. Now, do you want to work in the kitchen, or on deck? Even pirates must work!"

If you want to work below in the kitchen, turn to page 47.

If you want to do chores on deck, turn to page 55.

from page 25

You begin to dig up the wooden chest, but the pirates hear you, return, and tie you up next to the unconscious man. You may be on this island a long time.

THE END

You refuse to have anything to do with Captain Smith and his pirates. You walk swiftly off the plank, and splash into the warm ocean. You start swimming, hoping you can make it back to the beautiful island.

THE END

from page 74

Your sword-fighting ability has always saved you before, but this time you trust Rachel and her crystal. The light shines into the ogre's eyes. The monster's eyes turn violet, then red. The ogre staggers and turns into granite.

You banish the king and free all the prisoners. You are a hero, and can finally go home.

THE END

The cave is dark, but you see a light in a far corner. You follow the tunnel toward the light. Someone is holding a small torch. It is a dwarf, named Baldur, who has also taken refuge here.

Since you are both trying to get to the other side of the mountain, you decide to travel together. But already you must make a decision. Ahead of you the tunnel divides. To the left, the air seems slightly warmer, and you think you can hear tiny noises.

To the right, the air is cooler and the tunnel is silent.

If you want to take the left tunnel, turn to page 26.

If you want to take the right tunnel, turn to page 44.

from page 74

Your sword-fighting ability has gotten you through many scrapes, and you hope it can help you now. But the ogre is just too powerful. In the end, you too are captured.

THE END

You choose to help the leafers. If you survive, maybe they can help you later.

The leafers explain their problem. "An ogre has built a fortress in the deepest part of our forest. No one can wander freely with this beast living there. Many of us have been killed.

"We have tools, but we need someone like you with the courage to use them." They offer you a choice of weapons: A cap that lets you fly, or a cloak that makes you invisible.

If you want to take the cap, turn to page 64.

If you want to take the cloak, turn to page 76.

The tunnel to the right leads to an old wooden door with rusty iron braces. No one seems to have used the door for centuries. You try to listen for any noise inside, but you hear nothing.

If you want to try to break down this door, turn to page 81.

If you want to go back to the other tunnel, turn to page 26.

from page 6

You leap out of the open window (you look first, of course) onto a canopy that breaks your fall. You left just in time. You hear the door upstairs being broken down.

Now you have to decide fast. If you run, you may have time to catch the ship. Or you can try to slip quietly out of town and take the old forest road.

If you want to take the ship, turn to page 2.

If you want to take the forest road, turn to page 4.

from page 16

You would like to help the villagers, but the risks are just too great. You let the sailor go alone.

After only one hour, the nervous mutineers decide to begin their raid ahead of schedule. You wonder if the sailor made it to the village in time.

The ship sails quietly into port, only to be met by a surprise. Cannons fire at you from the shore. The villagers are ready. The sailor must have delivered his warning in time.

Your ship has to retreat. Away you sail, back to the open seas. You wonder if you will ever see your home again.

THE END

from page 35

You choose to work in the kitchen. It is boring work, peeling onions and washing the pirates' dishes. But one night after work you discover prisoners locked in the brig.

They are Captain Butler and his sailors. "Please free us," whispers Captain Butler. "Together we can overcome the pirates while they are sleeping."

It is a terrible risk for you. If the plan does not work, you will *all* walk the plank.

If you want to free the prisoners, turn to page 86.

If you think it is too dangerous to free them, turn to page 84.

48

At the top of the mountain, you meet a giant eagle. You tell him your story, and he is pleased that you have been killing huffers—his enemies. He offers you a ride. He can't take you all the way to your home —it is just too far. But he can take you to a nearby castle, or a nearby village, both in the next valley. He doesn't know, however, what you will find at either one.

If you want to be flown to the castle, turn to page 51.

If you want to be flown to the village, turn to page 61.

50

from page 16

You decide to help the sailor. As quietly as possible, while no one is looking, the two of you climb down a rope into the dark sea.

A mile is a long way to swim, but you are full of energy. By the time you reach the shore, you know you've made it in time to wake up the sleeping village. You have saved the town from a surprise attack. The people are grateful.

Tomorrow they give you a new ship on which you can travel home.

THE END

from page 48

You choose to go to the castle. You ask the eagle to land you in a secluded spot outside the castle wall. There you meet a young boy, who tells you that this castle belongs to evil King Hagborn. Hagborn has imprisoned many brave and honest citizens in the castle's dungeons. He is holding these people for ransom.

The boy asks you to free them. He takes you home with him and lends you his father's sword. The boy's father is one of King Hagborn's prisoners. Promising the boy that you will do your best to free the prisoners, you go outside again. The eagle is waiting for you.

If you want the eagle to land you in the castle's courtyard, turn to page 70.

If you want the eagle to fly you to the castle's tallest tower, turn to page 74.

The unidentified ship is a pirate ship. You are hauled aboard and brought before Captain Claudius Smith, the terror of the seas.

"How nice to have you," he growls. "We can certainly use you, and we will even give you a fair choice. Join our merry crew and become a pirate. Or walk the plank."

If you want to go along and say you will be a pirate, turn to page 35.

If you want to walk the plank, turn to page 37.

54

You keep the explosive hidden. The huffers take your sword away. They are very angry at you for killing their friends. They take you to their deepest tunnel and leave you in the lair of a horrible monster.

You only have a moment before the monster comes to eat you. The huffers run back up their tunnel in terror.

You prepare the explosive just before the monster looms out at you. You hide and the explosion kills the monster. Luckily, the blast opens a connection to a new tunnel. The huffers will be back soon, so you dash up this new tunnel. Though it is completely dark, the tunnel leads straight ahead and upward. Soon you feel a cool breeze. You emerge in bright sunlight at the top of the mountain.

Turn to page 48.

You decide to work on deck. It is difficult work, but you find you can handle it. A week later, it is your turn to be the lookout in the crow's nest. You are not up there long before you spot two powerful ships of the Royal Navy.

Don't they see you are a pirate ship? Why aren't they coming after you? Then you realize your ship is now flying the flag of a friendly nation.

If you want to think of some way to signal the navy, turn to page 90.

If you think it is too risky, turn to page 73.

from page 78

You do nothing. John Quince is led away by the guard, and you are left alone in your cell. Your meal for tonight, and for many nights to come, is gruel.

THE END

You don't think you will ever have another chance to use the explosive, so you set it off and hurl it toward the biggest huffer you see. It is the last thing you, and they, remember.

THE END

from page 69

You and Aleric enter Lokrin's cave that night.

"You have no business here," warns Lokrin.

"Great Lokrin," you say, "we are travelers who have heard of your wondrous helmet. Can it really turn you into any creature you desire? It seems so hard to believe."

Lokrin laughs and turns into a fire-spouting dragon.

Turn to page 29.

from page 78

Risking everything, you leap at the guard and take him by surprise. He does not even have a chance to cry out.

"Excellent," says John Quince. "That was just my plan. Now we can free the other prisoners. Working together, even the ogre cannot stop us. Tonight we will all be free!"

And you will be safely on your way home.

THE END

from page 48

You decide to go to the village. It is a glorious flight, high above the mountains and trees.

In the village, however, everyone looks pale. You stop at an inn, and learn that an evil wizard has cast a spell over the town.

A band of soldiers, led by Captain Sledge, plan to attack the wizard's castle this afternoon. You are invited to join them.

However, a man named Aleric tells you it is foolish to attack a wizard with swords. He knows a better way.

If you want to go with Captain Sledge and his soldiers, turn to page 66.

If you want to go with Aleric, turn to page 69.

You destroy the helmet, so that its power can never be misused in the future. The village is grateful to you, and they give you gold and a swift horse to make your journey home an easy one.

THE END

from page 26

It is too late to hide from the huffers. You and Baldur fight back bravely. Soon all the huffers lie dead. But your friend the dwarf has also fallen, mortally wounded. Before he dies, he gives you a magic explosive powder.

You barely have time to hide the powder in a pocket before a dozen more huffers appear. Walking slowly toward you, they are confident that they can now take you prisoner.

You could ignite the explosive. It would probably kill all the huffers. It might very well kill you, too.

If you want to surrender and keep the explosive hidden, turn to page 54.

If you want to take a chance on using the explosive, turn to page 57.

If you want to run from the huffers, turn to page 68.

64

from page 43

You take the cap and a sword from the leafers and fly off to the ogre's fortress. Hovering outside the bedroom window, you hear the ogre snoring inside.

If you want to try to kill the sleeping ogre with your sword, turn to page 72.

If you want to try to trick the ogre, turn to page 75.

66

There is often safety in numbers, so you go with Sledge and his soldiers. Your band marches right up to the front gate of the wizard's castle. Sledge bangs on the door and demands that the wizard either lift the spell or suffer the consequences.

A voice speaks from within. "Why do you bother an old man? Go away, or *you* may suffer."

Sledge quickly commands two of his soldiers to go around to the back of the castle. Then with his remaining soldiers, he prepares to break down the door.

If you want to attack with Sledge, turn to page 7.

If you want to join the two soldiers going around the back, turn to page 10.

You hide the helmet, in case you need to use it before you go home. You toy with the idea of living in the castle and ruling over the land yourself. But before you can decide, Aleric finds the helmet and begins to use it for his own evil purposes.

THE END

Down the dark tunnel you run, your torch lighting the way. Suddenly a rock trips you. You fall and the huffers grab you. The lights go out and there is a terrible hush.

THE END

You know it is foolhardy to attack a wizard, so you go with Aleric. He says the only way to defeat a wizard is by using even more powerful magic.

In the forest lives an old man who owns a great stolen treasure. It is not the treasure Aleric seeks, but the man's helmet. This magic helmet allows the man, named Lokrin, to change into whatever creature he wants.

Naturally this helmet gives Lokrin immense power. That is how he stole his hoard of treasure in the first place. But many years have passed since Lokrin has added to his wealth. Today he only stays in his cave and guards his treasure.

If you want to try to steal this helmet to defeat the wizard, turn to page 59.

If you want to go back with Captain Sledge, turn to page 66.

You land in the courtyard, but the king's guards take you prisoner. Your sword is taken away. You are led down to the dungeon and thrown into a filthy cell. But you are not alone. After the guards' footsteps die away, you meet your cellmate. His name is John Quince, son of the village baker. He is just finishing his meager meal.

"I have a plan to get out," says Quince, "but I need your help.

"When the guard comes to feed us, I'll pretend I'm sick. The guard will enter the cell—" John Quince does not have time to finish his plan, because suddenly you hear a guard's footsteps.

Turn to page 78.

from page 64

With your sword drawn, you quietly slip in through the ogre's bedroom window.

Unfortunately, the ogre's pipe yells, "Beware, master! A villain means to harm you!"

The ogre is a light sleeper. He wakes up, grabs you, and thinks you will make a delicious midnight snack.

THE END

You decide it is just too risky to warn the Royal Navy, so you remain silent.

The two ships sail by. It is your turn to wash the deck again. You may be scrubbing for a long time to come.

THE END

from page 51

The eagle lands you on the parapet of the tallest tower and waits there for you. You can see the mountains and immense forests in the distance.

Only one door leads inside the tower, so you carefully open the door.

Inside the room is a beautiful woman named Rachel, held prisoner by King Hagborn. She explains that a terrible ogre protects the king, and no one has been able to defeat the monster.

She asks you to help her and all the other prisoners held in the dungeons below. She gives you a crystal. "Shine the light from this crystal into the ogre's eyes, and he will turn to stone." You and Rachel go back outside, for that is the only way down, and the eagle gently lands you both outside the king's chamber.

You quietly enter the king's chamber, but he is waiting for you. King Hagborn looks at you and Rachel. "Fools!" he cries. The ogre leaps out from behind a stone column.

Can you trust Rachel's magic crystal?

If you want to fight the ogre with your sword, turn to page 41.

If you want to use the crystal, turn to page 38.

from page 64

Quietly you call through the open window to the snoring ogre, "Awake!" The ogre is instantly awake, but you are safely out of sight.

"Who dares to wake me?" asks the ogre.

"It is the north wind," you say, "and I have come to warn you."

"What are you talking about?" cries the ogre.

"Frost giants are down by your lake, and they mean to cause you great mischief."

With a terrible roar, the ogre storms out of his castle. At the lake he finds the giants, and fights them for seven hours. The mountains rumble with their battle. Then all is quiet. None of them are ever seen again.

The leafers can't stop thanking you. They will let you have any gift you desire. You take the cap, and use it to fly home.

THE END

76

from page 43

The cloak that makes you invisible will be most valuable. Slowly you make your way to the ogre's fortress. On the way, you pick up some rare herbs growing by a river.

The fortress guards never see you as you slip past them. In the dining room, the ogre's slaves are serving him dinner. You sneak up quietly beside the ogre, who is busily devouring his meal. You don't want to know what (or who) his dinner is.

"I am an invisible spirit," you whisper into the ogre's ear, "and I command you to stop eating." The ogre stops in mid-bite.

Turn to page 79.

from page 70

Your meal slides through the small opening at the bottom of the door.

Quince begins to groan. He is putting his plan into action. The suspicious guard comes into the room.

"If you're faking," he says to John Quince, "you'll be the next one we feed to the king's ogre."

If you want to try to overpower the guard, turn to page 60.

If you think it is too dangerous, turn to page 56.

"I command you to spill wine over your head," you tell the ogre. The ogre obeys you, and his slaves try not to giggle.

"Finally I command you to leave this place forever."

"Oh spirit," says the ogre. "I will gladly leave this forest. Only give me a sign—please just show yourself. I promise to do exactly as you say."

If you want to become visible for just a moment, turn to page 92.

If you choose to stay invisible, turn to page 88.

You break down the door. Your torch lights up the dusty room. Bottles, books, and wooden boxes are strewn all over. A second door stands at the other end of the room. You realize this may have once been the storage room of a wizard, for one book is full of spells.

Suddenly you hear the noise of pattering feet outside. Huffers—ferocious beings who spend most of their lives underground!

You have little time. Either you can take down two war axes that are mounted on the wall, or you can drink a clear potion that says it will let you see in the dark.

If you want to take the axes, turn to page 89.

If you want to take the "see-in-the-dark" potion, turn to page 87.

from page 10

First you tell the soldiers to stop. But they do not listen. They string their bows and prepare to shoot the magical animal.

You take a small knife from your pocket and quickly cut the men's bow strings before they can take aim. The men are angry at you, but you don't care.

The unicorn has wandered off into the woods, and you follow her. This is a day you will never forget. The unicorn allows you to ride her through the forest. It is the most wonderful experience of your life.

THE END

from page 47

You feel it is just too risky. You apologize to the Captain and go to your sleeping quarters.

As the days go by, you try not to think about the prisoners. One day, your ship is overtaken by a fleet from the Royal Navy. A great battle begins. Cannons roar, guns fire.

Finally the pirates surrender. Captain Butler and his sailors are freed, but you are taken back to port with the other pirates, to await trial for piracy on the high seas.

THE END

from page 47

You free the prisoners. That night you overpower the watchman and take over the ship. You lock Captain Smith and his pirates in their cabins, and sail the ship back to port.

With your share of the reward, you are able to take the next ship home, this time as a first-class passenger.

THE END

from page 81

To be able to see in the dark may be more useful than any weapon. You both drink the potion, and put out the torch. The potion works. You can see everything in the dark room clearly.

You have acted not a moment too soon. Huffers pour through the broken-down door. Then you realize that the spell may *not* be that useful. Maybe you can see in the dark, but the huffers have a torch that lights up the entire room. They can see you just fine!

The huffers howl in delight. But you have not lost hope yet. You know there is one more door at the other end of the room. You could make a run for it, or you could try to put out their torch with one of the many jars of water that lie on the floor.

If you want to make a run for the door, turn to page 34.

If you want to put out their torch, turn to page 23.

from page 79

You don't trust the ogre. You know he is trying to trick you. Remaining invisible, you take the special herbs you picked by the river and throw them one by one into the fire.

"Here is a sign," you say. "But I am growing impatient. You had better leave this forest right now."

The fire burns red, blue, and green, then explodes with a great burst of smoke. The slaves gasp. The ogre leaves his fortress forever.

That is the end of this adventure. If you wish, you can go home safely now, escorted by the leafers. Or you may climb the mountain path on your own.

If you want to climb the mountain, turn to page 30.

from page 81

You take the axes, and not a moment too soon. Huffers are howling outside the broken-down door. You and Baldur kill one, then another, but there are just too many. The brave dwarf falls.

With a sweeping ax blow, you kill three huffers at once. The remaining ones shriek, and run back in fear. You open the second door at the other end of the room, then lock it behind you. In this tunnel you feel a cool breeze. You dash up the tunnel for what seems like hours, and finally emerge in daylight. You are at the top of the mountain.

Turn to page 48.

90

from page 55

You try to think of some way to signal the navy. Your plan had better work or the pirates will surely feed you to the sharks.

Luckily the crow's nest has other kinds of flags stored away, including the Jolly Roger. You take down the friendly flag, and fly the skull and crossbones. It works!

The two Royal Navy ships sail toward you at top speed. It is too late for the pirates to stop you. They try to sail away, but the Royal Navy is too fast. They board your ship and take the pirates prisoner. You get a nice reward for your work and a free ride home.

THE END

from page 79

Since you have the ogre's promise, you figure it would be fun to show him how he has been fooled. You take off your cloak and reveal yourself. But the promise of an ogre is worthless. He grabs you before you can put your magic cloak back on, and you will be his dessert.

THE END